The Three Happy Lions

To Marc and Jacques

Also by Louise Fatio and illustrated by Roger Duvoisin

THE HAPPY LION

THE HAPPY LION IN AFRICA

THE HAPPY LION ROARS

THE HAPPY LION'S QUEST

THE HAPPY LION AND THE BEAR

LE BON LION

LE BON LION EN AFRIQUE

LES TROIS BONS LIONS

RED BANTAM

A DOLL FOR MARIE

FOURTH PRINTING

Library of Congress Catalog Card Number: 59-10706

THE

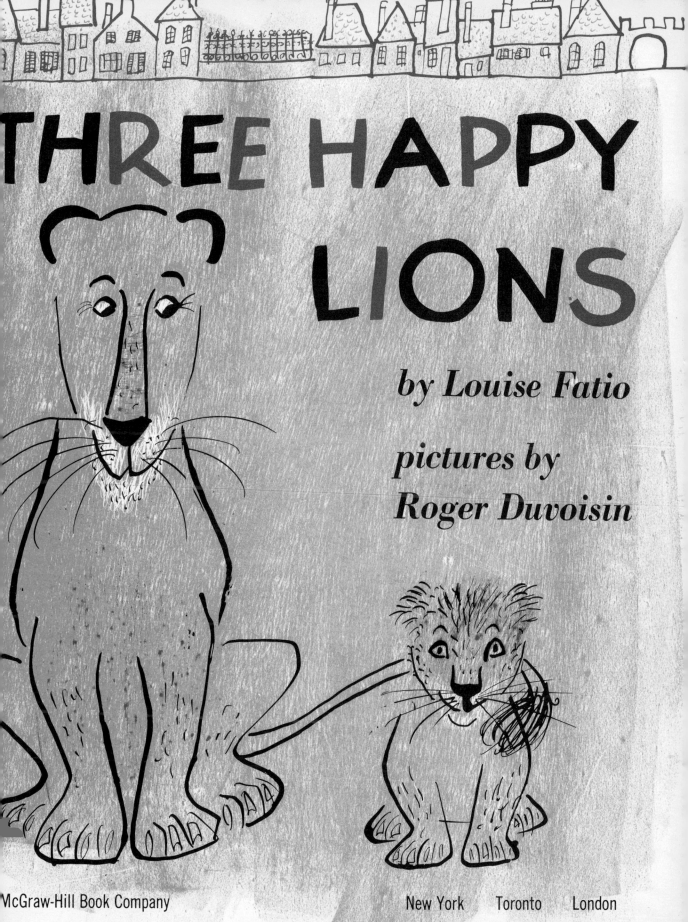

THREE HAPPY LIONS

by Louise Fatio

pictures by Roger Duvoisin

McGraw-Hill Book Company

New York Toronto London

There was once ONE Happy Lion
who lived in the zoo of a little French town.

Then there were TWO Happy Lions,
and that was better than one, for two are company.

Then . . . one day . . .
there were THREE HAPPY LIONS.
And that was even better than two, for the third Happy Lion

was a baby, so pretty and so playful
that all the children came to admire him.
"O, Maman," they cried, "*comme il est joli, le petit lion!*"

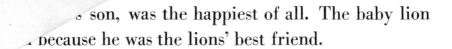
s son, was the happiest of all. The baby lion
because he was the lions' best friend.

Now, for once in his life, the first Happy Lion
had a frown over his eyes.
He was worried because he was a father.
"I am wondering," he said to the Lioness, "I am wondering,
aren't you, what trade we should give our son François
to keep him happy when he grows up?"
"He can be a pet, he is so gentle," answered the Lioness.
"That's a capital quality for a pet."
"Why not a circus lion? He is so clever and strong," said the Happy Lion.
"Why not a zoo lion like us, he is so handsome to look at?"

"Well," sighed the Happy Lion, "there do not seem to
be any other trades for lions, do there? I never saw a lion policeman."

"Nor a lion fireman."

"Nor a lion schoolteacher."

LA SOURIS
LE CHAT
LE CHIEN

"If you want my opinion," said the Happy Lion,
"this is an upside-down world. Think of all the things
a clever lion could do."

Now one day, while the Happy Lion was still wondering,
there came to visit the zoo a rich lady with beautiful furs
and gold necklaces. She exclaimed at once:
"*O, quel mignon petit lion!* May I have him for a pet?
I would love him so."
The Happy Lion and the Lioness shed some tears
when the lady was allowed to take François with her,
but after all, it was time for him to learn a trade.

It was thus that François became a pet.

The rich lady lived in a splendid house with silk curtains
at every window and thick rugs on which François' paws
padded silently.
She bought him a red ribbon to tie around his neck
and a coat to keep him warm on afternoon walks.
Every morning, while the lady was eating her breakfast in bed,
François rolled and played like a kitten on her lace and silk bed quilt.
"Mon gentil petit lion," the lady would say,
"you are the darlingest pet." And she would kiss him on his black nose.

It was a pleasant life and François liked it well enough.
He grew fat and round, and so big that he could soon jump
by himself onto the lady's bed quilt.

And he grew

and grew

and grew

until one morning, as he jumped onto the bed quilt—

CRASH, the bed broke in two!

"*O, quelle horreur, mon petit lion, comme tu es gros!*"
cried the lady. "How sad it is that a pet baby lion
cannot remain a baby lion!"

"My darling François," she added with a tear, "I will not
be able to keep you as a pet. I will give you to my friend
Monsieur Tambour, the circus owner. He will love you too,
and will teach you wonderful tricks."

And it was thus that François became a circus lion.

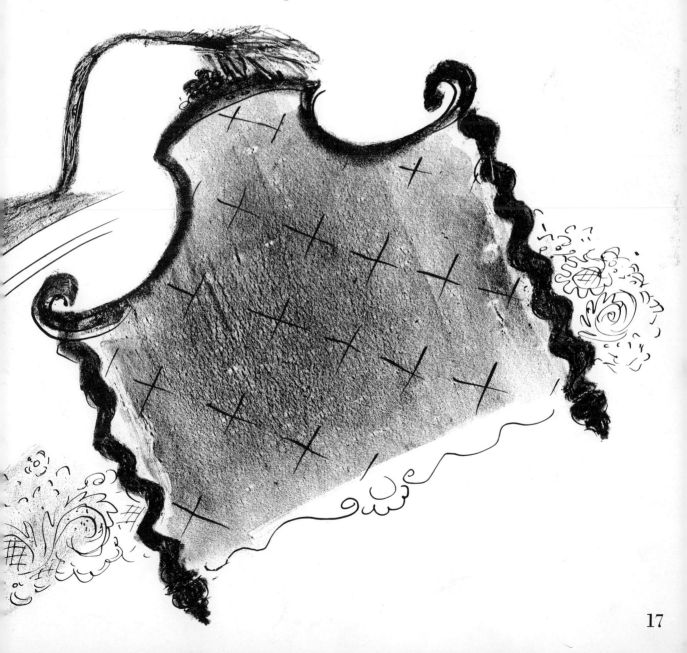

At first François thought that the circus was much like the zoo.
There were two snarling tigers, two bears, two elephants, two seals.
But animals are not taught tricks in the zoo.
They are in the circus.   And that makes all the difference.
The tigers roared from the top of a high stool.
The bears rode bicycles.   The elephants danced.
The seals played the trumpets.

"Mon ami," said Monsieur Tambour to François, "you will jump through a hoop of fire. And you will learn to roar ferociously and swish your tail angrily. You will walk the way the King of Wild Beasts must walk. That is what you are, after all. It will give goose pimples to people, and that's why they come to the circus."
At once the lessons began. To teach François, Monsieur Tambour walked and roared like the King of Beasts, and with his arms he showed how an angry lion's tail swished. "Right, like this . . . left, like that . . . up and down.

That's a mighty angry tail.
People must fear that you are going to eat me up!"
But no part of François could look angry,
not even his tail, however hard he tried.
"*O, la, la!*" exclaimed Monsieur Tambour. "*Pas comme ça, mon ami!*
You look as gentle as a lady's poodle. No one will have goose pimples
looking at you or hearing you. Now, hear *my* roar:
RRRRRRROOOOOOOOAAAAAARRRRRRR . . ."
went Monsieur Tambour. It was so frightening that François
did have goose pimples.

The lessons went thus every day, and Monsieur Tambour
looked and sounded more and more ferocious.
But not so François.
"Why should I look ferocious," he wondered.
"I do not want to eat Monsieur Tambour!"
After many lessons, Monsieur Tambour gave up. He had to,
for he had lost his voice trying to roar louder and louder.

24

"Never mind, *mon ami*," he whispered. "You are the sweetest
King of Wild Beasts I have ever seen.   But that won't do in the circus.
Now let's see if you can do the flaming hoop trick."
Now François did like to play with hoops, but not flaming ones.
Weren't such things rather silly? When something
was burning at the zoo, the firemen came to put the fire out!
No, François would have none of it.

Hereupon Monsieur Tambour said, "*Mon ami,* you will never make a circus performer. If you ask me, I think you should go back to the zoo."

"I would rather," thought François. "I do not like

to give goose pimples to people. I like people."
So Monsieur Tambour took François back to the friendly zoo.
The Happy Lion and the Lioness were so happy to embrace him
that they did not mind at all
his having failed to remain a pet and a circus lion.
But François knew all along that there was something else
he wanted to do.

Now a zoo is a very busy place, as everyone knows who has lived in one.
There are children riding the zebra.   Parents watching them.
Nurses pushing baby carriages.   Soldiers, policemen, and lovers
walking in the shaded paths.   And the animals in their houses
and gardens.
But ever since he was a baby lion, François had especially loved
to watch the other François—François the keeper's son.
This François had become a helper to the park gardener
and looked so contented as he planted and watered flowers
and made the walks neat with his rake
that François the lion had decided long ago
he wanted to be a gardener too.
Think of living and working among brilliant and scented flowers!

So François the lion set out to help François the gardener.
With what ease he pushed the wheelbarrow loaded with pots of flowers!
Dig a hole for a tree? No one did that better than he.

Water the flowers? How amusing.
Weed the flower beds? Rake the leaves? Spray the flowers for bugs?
Just the right work for a lion!

In no time François the lion became such a good gardener
and could make flowers grow so fine that the Mayor decided
OFFICIALLY that the park needed two gardener's helpers—
the two François.

And thus it was that François the lion became a gardener.
The Happy Lion and the Lioness were now very pleased
with their son. They spent many happy hours watching
the two François work like two good friends to make the park
more beautiful than it had ever been.

"Show us another lion who has ever been a gardener,"
said the Happy Lion. "It's just as I said before,
there *are* other trades for clever lions."